To my parents, who never told me
my dreams were nonsense.

G. M.

First published 2015 by Macmillan Children's Books,
an imprint of Pan Macmillan
a division of Macmillan Publishers Limited
20 New Wharf Road, London N1 9RR
Basingstoke and Oxford
Associated companies throughout the world
www.panmacmillan.com

ISBN: 978-0-230-76590-0 (HB)
ISBN: 978-1-4472-1488-5 (PB)

Text and illustrations copyright © Gemma Merino 2015
Moral rights asserted.

1 3 5 7 9 8 6 4 2

A CIP catalogue record for this book is available from the British Library.

Printed in China

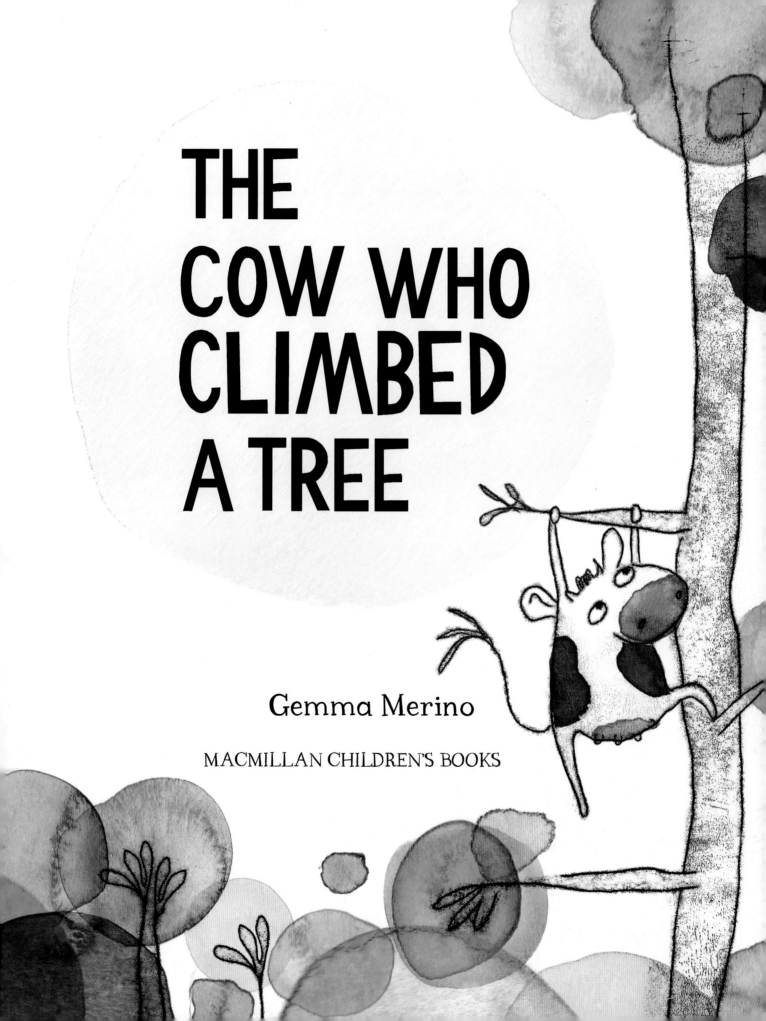

THE
COW WHO
CLIMBED
A TREE

Gemma Merino

MACMILLAN CHILDREN'S BOOKS

Tina was a very curious cow.
She had a thirst for discovery.

Her mind was full of wonderful things,
all of which her sisters found very silly.

"IMPOSSIBLE!
RIDICULOUS!
NONSENSE!"
they would say every time she told them her
amazing ideas.

Her sisters were only
interested in one thing:
fresh and juicy grass.

One day when Tina was exploring the woods,

she decided to try something new.

She began
to climb
a tree.

Up and up
she went.

And at the top?
Tina couldn't believe her eyes.

Unlike the fierce dragons she had seen in her books, this one was friendly . . .

and vegetarian.

All afternoon they talked about wonderful dreams and incredible stories.

Tina couldn't wait to tell
her sisters about her new friend.

But her sisters were NOT impressed.

"Dragons don't exist.

Cows can't climb trees.

IMPOSSIBLE! RIDICULOUS!

NONSENSE!" they said.

And with that they went to bed.

But the next morning,

Tina was nowhere to be seen.

Her sisters found a note.

Well, that was it!

Tina's nonsense had gone too far.

The sisters decided to go and find her and bring her home.

For the first time, they ventured beyond the farm and into the woods.

They had never imagined it
would be so beautiful . . .

And then they came across something very strange.

"IMPOSSIBLE!" they said.

FLYING LESSONS TODAY

But the first cow
began to climb, and
one after another,
up they went.

The world beyond the fields
was extraordinary.

But where was Tina?
Suddenly the cows looked up . . .

It was IMPOSSIBLE.
It was RIDICULOUS.
It was NONSENSE.

But it was TRUE!

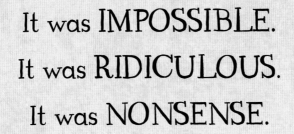

Tina was FLYING!

And when she asked her sisters to join her,
they said something they had never said before . . .

And after that, they just couldn't
wait to see what else was possible.